Paddington

in Hot Water

Paddington

MICHAEL BOND

in Hot Water

Illustrated by R.W. Alley

Collins

An imprint of HarperCollinsPublishers

One evening Paddington announced he
was going up to his room because he had
some important postcards to write.

After saying goodnight to everyone, he went into the kitchen and made himself some marmalade sandwiches in case he became hungry.

As soon as he arrived upstairs he put the sandwiches away for safe keeping, then changed into his pyjamas before starting work on a postcard to his Aunt Lucy.

First he wrote the address: Aunt Lucy, Home
for Retired Bears, Lima, Peru, then he added
the stamp. As usual, Paddington had a lot to
tell his aunt and
he wanted to
make sure there
was plenty of
room on
the card.

Dear Aunt Lucy,

Aunt Lucy
Home for Retired
Bears,
Lima, Peru

Aunt Lucy's postcard took much longer than
he had bargained for, and by the time he'd
finished he felt ready for a sandwich.
The trouble was he couldn't remember
where he had put them.

He looked
under the bed.

He looked on top
of the wardrobe.

He looked in his
dressing table
drawers

and he looked
behind the curtains.

He even looked
under his pillow in
case he had hidden
them there by
mistake, but they
were nowhere to
be seen.

In the end Paddington went to bed hungry.
In the past he had often found that if you
fell asleep with something on your mind,
you dreamt about it. And sure enough, that
night his dreams were full of marmalade.
Everywhere he looked there
was marmalade.

There were great orange mountains of it,
rows of giant jars, and golden chunks piled so
high he needed a ladder to climb over them.

There was even a moment when he found
himself wading through a crocodile-infested
swamp up to his waist in marmalade.

"Are you all right, dear?" asked Mrs Brown, when she went into his room the next morning. "I thought I heard you calling out during the night."

"I was being chased by a crocodile," said Paddington. "It's left me feeling very sticky, so I think I may have a bath."

"I do hope Paddington's all right," said Mrs Brown when she arrived downstairs. "He's having a bath without being asked."

"Well, I hope he wipes himself dry," said Mrs Bird. "We shall never hear the last of it if he catches a cold with the shock."

Meanwhile, Paddington was just climbing into the bath. Unfortunately, his mind was still so full of his dreams he forgot to remove his pyjamas.

It wasn't long before he discovered that taking pyjamas off when they are dry is one thing, but trying to do it in a bath full of hot, soapy water is quite another matter.

The more he struggled, the harder it became, until there was more water on the floor than there was in the bath.

In fact, there was so
much water lying
around he had to use
all the spare bath towels
in order to mop it up.
And when he ran out
of towels he started on
the linen cupboard.
Very soon he had
used up so many
pillowcases, sheets
and dressing gowns,
the bathroom looked
just like the inside
of a laundry.

Later that morning Mrs Brown happened to glance out of the dining room window.

"Well I never," she said. "Paddington's not only had a bath without being asked, but it looks as though he's done the week's washing as well! I wonder what's come over him?"

"If you ask me," said Mrs Bird, "that bear's been up to something he'd rather we didn't know about. Perhaps," she added wisely, "it's best not to ask. We shall find out soon enough."

Which was just as
well for Paddington,
because he was
about to make
another discovery.
Worn out by all
his labours, he
climbed back into

bed, and as he did so his feet came up against
something cold and sticky.

Rolling back the bedclothes
he found where he had
left his marmalade
sandwiches the
night before.

"Oh, dear!" he exclaimed to the world in
general. "I think I may need another bath!"
Paddington gave a deep sigh as he hurried along
the landing carrying his bedclothes.

Sometimes getting up in the morning could
take all day.

First published in Great Britain by HarperCollins*Publishers* in 2000
This enlarged paperback edition first published by Collins Picture Books in 2002

1 3 5 7 9 8 6 4 2

ISBN: 0 00 710765 X

Text copyright © Michael Bond 2000
Illustrations copyright © R.W. Alley 2000

A CIP catalogue record for this title is available from the British Library.

The HarperCollins website address is: www.**fire**and**water**.com

Printed and bound in Hong Kong

Paddington titles in paperback include:

Paddington Bear
Paddington at the Carnival
Paddington and the Christmas Surprise
Paddington at the Circus
Paddington the Artist
Paddington at the Zoo
Paddington at the Fair
Paddington and the Tutti Frutti Rainbow
Paddington at the Palace